Little Fox
Goes to the
End of the World

A story by Ann Tompert

With pictures by John Wallner

Crown Publishers, Inc., New York

The text of this book is set in 16 pt. Baskerline.
The illustrations are black pencil drawings with pencil shaded overlays
prepared by the artist and printed in four colors.

Library of Congress Cataloging in Publication Data
Tompert, Ann.
   Little fox goes to the end of the world.
   Summary: Little Fox tells her mother all the frightening things
she'll see and do when she travels to the end of the world.
   I. Wallner, John C.   II. Title.
PZ7.T598Li3   [E]   75-44381
ISBN 0-517-52600-X

For Norma Jean

J.C.W.

Little Fox was chasing a butterfly. Her
mother sat nearby, sewing her a new jacket.
Farther and farther Little Fox strayed.

"Come back, Little Fox," called her mother,
"or you may get lost."

Little Fox walked back to her mother ever
so slowly. She was tired of playing in the soft
green grass near the mouth of her den.

"Someday," she said, "I'm going to travel to
   the end of the world."
"Oh," said her mother, "is the end of the world
   very far?"

"Yes," said Little Fox. "It is very very far. I will
have to go through a deep forest to get to it."
"Won't you get lost?" asked her mother.

"Oh, no," said Little Fox. "I will carry a lantern."
"What will you see?" asked her mother.

"Bears!" exclaimed Little Fox.

"Oh, dear!" cried her mother, dropping
the jacket and covering her eyes.
"Won't you be scared?"

"No," laughed Little Fox. "I like bears.
I'll take a pot of honey along and give
some to each bear I meet."

"That's a good idea," said her mother.
"I would not have thought of that.
 What else will you see?"

"Tigers!" shouted Little Fox. "They will roar
and growl and try to scare me!"
"I'd hide," exclaimed her mother.

"Not me," said Little Fox. "I'll take my drum
and I'll beat it as loud as I can.
I'll scare THEM away!"
"I'm glad," said her mother.

"But the noise will scare the elephants.
They will come charging after me."
"I'd be scared," said her mother.

"Not me," said Little Fox.
"I'll take a ladder so I can climb
  up a tree."
"You will be safe there,"
  said her mother.
"No, I won't," said Little Fox.
"There will be monkeys in the
  tree and they won't like
  my being there."

"Oh, my goodness!" said her mother.
"Don't worry," said Little Fox. "I'll take
some bananas. They will like that."

"Is the end of the world in the forest?"
asked her mother.
"Oh, no," laughed Little Fox. "I will have to
leave the forest and cross the mountains.
They will be covered with snow."
"Will it be hard?" asked her mother.

"Yes," said Little Fox. "And the snow will
be deep. The icy winds will try to freeze me."

Little Fox's mother shivered and wrapped
her shawl around her.
"But I'll run like the wind," said Little Fox.

"And you will have your jacket to keep you warm," said her mother as she put it on her to see how it would fit. "Then will you be at the end of the world?"

"No," said Little Fox. "I will have to cross the hot desert, but I'll take father's old umbrella to protect me from the sun."

"Then will you be at the end of the world?"
asked her mother.
"Oh, no," said Little Fox. "I will have to cross
a river filled with crocodiles. They'll be
waiting to gobble me up."
Little Fox's mother gasped.

"Don't worry," said Little Fox. "I'll take my boat
and, if you lend me your broom, I'll sweep
the crocodiles out of my way and sail down
the river to the open sea."
"You will be safe then," said her mother.

"Only if I may borrow your clothesline and
four pillowcases," said Little Fox.
"What for?" asked her mother.
"To make a lasso and capture the Four Winds.
Then I will put each wind in a separate bag."

"But how will you sail with no wind?"
asked her mother.

"I'll let the East Wind out. It will fill my sails and send me toward the end of the world," said Little Fox.

"That will be nice," said her mother.

"Oh, no, it won't. The East Wind will blow up
a storm. It will rock and roll my boat
and try to smash it against the rocks."
Little Fox's mother threw her apron over her head.

"But I'll let the West Wind out," said Little Fox.
"It will blow my boat away from the rocks."
"Good," said her mother. "You will be safe then."

"No, I won't," said Little Fox. "It will blow me into
the island of the One-eyed Cats."

"That sounds awful!" cried her mother.
"What will you do?"
"I'll let the South Wind out," said Little Fox.
"Its gentle breeze will blow me to the end
  of the world."

"At last," said her mother. She put on
Little Fox's jacket and buttoned it up.
"But I shall miss you."

"And I shall miss you," said Little Fox.
"So I'll let out the North Wind and head
  straight for home."
"And I shall be waiting for you with your
  favorite dinner," said her mother.

Date Due